THE TRIALS OF WASTELAND

By

Tegh Munjral Karla

Published in 2025

To the ones who ask questions when the world goes
quiet.
To the ones who follow the clues even when the
truth hurts.
And to the ones who never stop searching—
this story is yours.

Some stories begin with a character. Mine began with a question:

What if the person you trust the most is the one hiding everything?

The Trials of Wasteland is a story that refused to stay quiet in my head. It whispered secrets, revealed clues, and asked impossible questions until I had no choice but to follow. What began as a simple mystery unfolded into something much bigger—a tangled web of trust, betrayal, and the terrifying power of truth.

This isn't just a book about a death. It's about what dies inside us when we're forced to question everything we thought we knew. It's about people who get too close to the truth and others who run from it. It's about a wasteland—not just the one around us, but the one within us.

If you're here, reading this, you've already entered the first trial.

Keep your eyes open.

Nothing is what it seems.

— Teg Munjral

Preface

Every mystery hides more than one truth.
At first glance, this is a story about two brave cops, a curious group of kids, and a world full of secrets waiting to be uncovered. But as you turn the pages, you'll find that not everything or everyone is what they seem.
When one of the officers, Lou, is found dead under strange circumstances, the journey takes a wild turn.
The group's desperate search leads them across unexpected paths, even into another universe. But even then, the real danger remains hidden in plain sight.
In this book, trust is fragile, clues are everywhere, and betrayal runs deeper than anyone can imagine.
Prepare for twists, turns, and a story that reminds us: sometimes, the biggest mystery isn't where someone has gone, but who they truly are.

This book would not exist without the fearless guidance and faith of our mentor, *Ridhhima Mohan*, who believed in my voice when I was still finding it. Thank you for challenging me, cheering me on, and giving me the space to create without fear.
To my family—thank you for always believing in me, for the quiet comfort, and the loud celebrations.

To our readers, friends, and fellow dreamers: this is for you.

The Hunter's Moon

Cincinnati lay under a suffocating blanket of darkness, the town's lights extinguished as if by some malevolent force. The air was thick with an unsettling silence, broken only by the distant, mournful hoot of an owl. A young boy named Paul, with pale ivory skin, pimples, and braces, darted through the dense forest, his heart pounding like a drum in his chest. Shadows seemed to reach out from the trees, clawing at him as he ran. Despite his fear, Paul's sharp mind raced with thoughts of escape, drawing on the mystery novels he loved so much.

Behind him, a man in a white dotted shirt, a coat, and a tie followed, a glinting knife in his hand, reflecting the faint, eerie moonlight. This man, known only as "The Stalker," was Cincinnati's most ruthless and deranged killer. His calm demeanour and meticulous nature made him a terrifying predator. Desperate and terrified, Paul vaulted into a green, acrid dumpster. He held his breath, surrounded by the stench of garbage, fighting the urge to gag. The killer, panting heavily, approached the dumpster but, without peeking inside, moved on, his footsteps echoing ominously in the still night.

Paul had narrowly escaped the clutches of The Stalker. Once the man left, Paul sprinted towards the police station, his mind clouded with fear and anxiety. The station was dilapidated, with cramped walls and rusted doors, adding to the sense of dread. His story made the police officer,

Lou, a chiselled man with a few strands of hair and black-beady eyes, sigh in exasperation. Lou was a seasoned officer, known for his no-nonsense attitude and dedication to his job. However, he was also irritable and tired, overwhelmed with cases. "Can't believe Roger had to take a leave today," he muttered.

"Officer, please, you have to help me! I was just being hunted by a man! He had a knife! I flew from London this morning for a fan meet-up. I never imagined I'd be nearly murdered," Paul stammered, his voice trembling and eyes wide with terror. Lou, skeptical, looked at his constable and scoffed. "I've had enough teens playing pranks today," he said. "Where are your parents, kid?"

Paul, still shaken, explained that he had been dropped off at Heathrow Airport by his parents for his flight to Cincinnati. Lou, glancing at the clock, realized how late it was and how his family was waiting for him at home for Thanksgiving dinner. "I can't find my phone, my ID, or my wallet. They must have been stolen by the man who was following me," Paul said, his voice trembling.

Before Lou could respond, the station's phone rang. It was a report of a break-in at a nearby store. Lou instructed his constable to handle it, but the interruption gave him a moment to think. "Alright, kid, let's get you somewhere safe for now," Lou said, his tone softening slightly. "I'll drop you off at your hotel. We'll discuss this more tomorrow." Paul agreed and was dropped off at The Lancabala Hotel.

Before Lou could head home, two more kids, Jamie and Ada, rushed into the station, claiming they were being followed and mugged. Jamie, with her fiery eyes and determined stance, spoke first. "Officer, we need help! A man was following us, and he tried to take our bags!" Ada, clutching her friend's arm, nodded vigorously, her eyes wide with fear. "We were separated from our parents at the airport. We don't know where they are," Jamie explained, her voice shaking. "We tried calling them, but we couldn't reach them," Ada added, her voice barely above a whisper.

Lou, now more concerned, asked for details. "Where did this happen?" he inquired gently. Jamie explained, "Around 5:30, on the outskirts of Ackmore Street, outside Barry's joke shop. The mugger wore a brown coat with a skull sign and some Latin saying." Lou filed their report and dropped them off at the hotel. As he returned to the station, two more boys, Marcos and Ian, entered, claiming a man had chased them. Marcos, with a determined look in his eyes, took charge of the conversation. "Officer, we were just chased by a man with a knife. He had a Nazi symbol tattoo and mentioned 'Carl,' the influencer's real name," he said. Standing slightly behind Marcos, Ian added, "It happened around 5:32 pm on Ackmore Street."

Lou's mind raced with the connections between the incidents. He couldn't shake the feeling that something much larger and more sinister was at play. As he drove home, the shadows seemed to close in around him, and a sense of impending doom settled over him. He knew that the next day would bring more revelations, and possibly more danger.

The Silent Menace

Lou parked his Ford and exited, muttering, "A couple of kids came by today, reported similar incidents. Never heard of that gaming guy." His mind was a whirlpool of worry, the unsettling events of the day gnawing at him. The thought of food was far from his mind as he approached his front door. His wife, Griselda, called out, "Dinner's ready, Lou!" The mention of food brought a fleeting sense of relief, a small comfort in the chaos.

He decided to text Roger, his long-time partner and best friend. They had been through thick and thin together, their bond forged in the fires of countless cases. "Hey Roger, just got home. A couple of kids came by today, reported similar incidents. Something's off. Hope you're feeling better," he typed quickly before stepping inside.

"Hey kids, how was your day?" he asked, trying to mask his worry with a smile. His red-haired twins, Larry and Lorry, were excited for Thanksgiving. "Kids, it's time to say your prayers," Lou said. They prayed, and Lou savoured his wife's turkey, the familiar flavours grounding him momentarily.

After dinner, Lou's thoughts returned to Roger. "Griselda, can you pack some food for Roger? He's not well, and I know he probably hasn't eaten," he said. Griselda nodded, understanding the unspoken bond between the two men. Lou then called one of his neighbours, asking them to deliver the food to Roger's place.

Lou and Roger had been partners for over a decade, their camaraderie built on mutual respect and shared experiences. They had solved numerous cases together, their skills complementing each other perfectly. Lou's intuition and Roger's analytical mind made them an unstoppable team. They had each other's backs, both on and off duty, and their friendship had grown stronger with each passing year.

The next morning, Lou scrubbed the dishes while jamming to jazz music. He then woke his kids with raucous rock music, making them groan. "Alright kids, freshen up, I've prepared nut muffins for breakfast," he said. The kids groaned again, but were delighted to find chocolate chip pancakes instead. Lou, a natural comedian, used a pancake as a puppet, making his kids laugh. Griselda, woken by the laughter, joined them, turning on some music.

Lou dropped his kids at the bus stop before heading to the police station. "Hey Roger, glad you made it today," Lou greeted his colleague. Roger, with his swarthy skin and chiselled face, replied, "Yet, I still get more assignments done." The day passed with Lou and Roger researching the influencer and similar cases.

As they sifted through the reports, Lou's eyes widened. "Roger, look at this," he said, his voice trembling slightly. "All the parents of these kids... they're dead. Every single one of them, the day after the kids left for Cincinnati."

Roger's face paled. "What the hell, Lou? This can't be a coincidence. We need to dig deeper. There's something really messed up going on here."

Lou nodded, his mind racing. "Let's gather all the files and look for more connections. We need to figure out what's happening before more kids get hurt."

They realized that the secret records they needed were kept with the chief, and accessing them required special permission. Lou volunteered to go to the chief's office to gather the files. "I'll handle this, Roger. You stay here and keep an eye on things. We can't afford to leave the station unattended," Lou said.

Roger agreed, though reluctantly. "Be careful, Lou. This whole thing is giving me the creeps."

Lou had to visit the chief's office alone, as Roger had to stay behind to manage the station. After a long drive, he arrived at the chief's office. The receptionist, sitting in a squeaky chair, asked for his ID. Lou handed it over, and she examined it carefully. "The chief will see you in 30 minutes," she said. Lou waited in the silent, all-white room. A young officer brought him a cup of tea, which he sipped slowly, trying to calm his nerves.

When the chief, Lydia, arrived, Lou explained his need for the records. Lydia, a five-foot-tall woman with curly hair, listened intently. "I'm sorry, Lou, but those records are classified. The kids are related to influential people, and we can't release that information," she said firmly. Lou felt a wave of frustration but knew better than to argue. "I understand, Chief. Thanks for your time," he said, standing up. As he turned to leave, Lydia added, "Be careful, Lou. There's more to this than meets the eye." Lou nodded, the weight of her words adding to his growing sense of unease.

As Lou walked out of the office, a sudden chill ran down his spine. The hallway seemed darker, the shadows deeper. He felt a presence behind him, but when he turned, there was nothing. His heart pounded as he hurried to his car, the feeling of being watched growing stronger with each step. He fumbled with his keys, finally managing to unlock the door and slide into the driver's seat. He took a deep breath, trying to shake off the eerie sensation.

Driving home, the roads seemed unusually deserted. The streetlights flickered, casting long, sinister shadows. Lou's mind raced with thoughts of the cases, the dead parents, and the ominous warning from Lydia. He couldn't shake the feeling that something terrible was about to happen.

As he pulled into his driveway, his phone buzzed. It was a message from an unknown number: "You can't escape the truth, Lou. It's closer than you think." His blood ran cold. He looked around, but the street was empty. The message sent a wave of dread through him, and he quickly entered his house, locking the door behind him.

Inside, the house was eerily quiet. Lou's family was already asleep. He checked on his kids, their peaceful faces a stark contrast to the turmoil in his mind. He went to his room, but sleep eluded him. The events of the day played over and over in his head, each detail more disturbing than the last.

Suddenly, a loud crash echoed through the house. Lou jumped out of bed, grabbing his gun from the nightstand. He crept down the hallway, his heart pounding in his chest. The noise had come from the kitchen. He moved silently, his senses on high alert. As he entered the kitchen, he saw the back door wide open, the cold night air blowing in.

Lou's eyes scanned the room, but there was no sign of an intruder. He closed the door and locked it, his mind racing. He turned to leave, but a shadow moved in the corner of his eye. He spun around, gun raised, but there was nothing there. The room was empty.

A sudden dizziness washed over him, and he stumbled, clutching the counter for support. His vision blurred, and he felt a cold hand on his shoulder. He turned, but there was no one there. Panic set in as his legs gave way, and he collapsed to the floor. The last thing he heard before darkness claimed him was a whisper in his ear, "Yes boss, the job is done."

The Grim Discovery

The morning sun cast long shadows over the desolate lake, its surface a mirror of murky secrets. Roger, a seasoned detective with a rugged face and piercing blue eyes, stood at the edge, his breath visible in the crisp air. He couldn't shake the nagging worry about Lou's whereabouts. Lou hadn't checked in since the previous night, and Roger's gut told him something was wrong.

Earlier that morning, a local fisherman had reported seeing a car careen off the road and plunge into the lake. The lake was massive, its dark waters stretching out like an abyss. Roger and his team had rushed to the scene, their mission clear: find the car and retrieve any occupants. The air was thick with tension as they prepared to pull the vehicle from the depths.

"Come on, guys! We're running out of time. Let's hurry up and pull this car out," Roger shouted, his voice echoing through the stillness. The winch groaned under the strain as the car slowly emerged from the water, its windows shattered and body covered in algae. Jim, a tall man with a ponytail and a weathered face, suddenly shouted, "Oh Roger!" His voice was tinged with urgency and dread.

Roger turned, his heart sinking as he saw the bloated, discolored body inside the car. His stomach churned as he recognized the familiar features. It was Lou. Without hesitation, he jumped into the lake, the cold water biting at his skin. He broke the remaining glass and pulled Lou's lifeless body from the wreckage. Lou's head was twisted at an unnatural angle, his eyes staring blankly, giving him an unwanted view of his own buttocks.

The sight was horrifying, but Roger's mind was already racing. He had to find out what had happened. As he climbed out of the water, his hands trembled as he checked Lou's phone, hoping for some clue. There, on the screen, was a message from Griselda: "Lou, don't forget to pick up the kids after school. Love you." The normalcy of the message contrasted starkly with the grim reality before him.

The words hit Roger like a punch to the gut. He sank to his knees beside Lou's body, the weight of grief and guilt overwhelming him. Tears streamed down his face as he clutched Lou's cold hand, his mind a whirlwind of emotions. "Why, Lou? Why did this happen?" Roger whispered, his voice breaking. The sight of his best friend, lifeless and broken, was too much to bear. He felt a deep, aching sorrow mixed with a burning need for answers. Roger was filled with guilt, feeling he should have been there to protect Lou, to prevent this tragedy.

Roger's sobs echoed across the lake, his body shaking with the intensity of his grief. He had always been the strong one, the one who held everything together, but now he felt utterly shattered. The memories of their years together, the cases they had solved, the laughs they had shared, all came flooding back, making the pain even more unbearable.

After composing himself, Roger knew he had to face Lou's family. He drove to Lou's house, the journey feeling like an eternity. When he arrived, he saw a police car parked outside. Another officer, who had been sent to inform the family, was just leaving. Griselda opened the door, her eyes red and swollen from crying. Roger embraced her, his own tears mingling with hers. "I'm so sorry, Griselda," he whispered, his voice choked with emotion.

Griselda broke down in his arms, her sobs wracking her body. "Why, Roger? Why did this happen to Lou?" she cried. Roger had no answers, only a deep, aching sorrow. He hugged Lou's kids, their innocent faces filled with confusion and grief. "I'll find out what happened. I promise," he said, his voice filled with determination.

Descending the stairs to the basement of the police station later that day, Roger's hands trembled as he found a note labelled "Lou's Final Adieu." His heart pounded as he read Lou's confession of involvement in a murder. The words blurred as tears filled his eyes. Overwhelmed by guilt and grief, Roger knew he had to act quickly. He decided not to tell Griselda or the family about the note, not wanting to add to their pain.

Roger decided to visit the hotel where the kids involved in the case were staying. The drive was a blur, his mind replaying the events of the past few days. The hotel loomed ahead, its facade casting eerie shadows in the fading light. Roger's footsteps echoed in the empty hallway as he approached the room.

Inside, the kids were huddled together, their faces pale with fear. Paul, the oldest, stepped forward. "Officer, what's going on? We heard about Lou. Is it true?" His voice was shaky, but there was a determination in his eyes.

Roger took a deep breath. "We discovered Lou's remains and a farewell letter. Have you seen anything unusual recently?" he asked, his voice steady but filled with sorrow.

The kids shook their heads, their eyes wide with innocence. "No, we haven't," Jamie said, her voice barely above a whisper. "We've been at the hotel the whole time."

Paul, ever the thinker, suggested, "Maybe we can help you, Officer. We need to clear our names and find out what really happened."

Roger shook his head, his voice heavy with grief. "No, it's too dangerous. I can't involve you in this."

"But we might know something that could help," Paul insisted, his eyes pleading. "Please, let us try."

Roger hesitated, the weight of his decision pressing down on him. He was about to refuse again when Jamie spoke up, her voice trembling. "We saw something...

something strange near the hotel. We didn't think it was important at the time, but now..."

Roger's heart skipped a beat. "What did you see?" he asked, his voice barely above a whisper.

Jamie exchanged a glance with Paul before continuing. "There was a man, dressed in black. He was watching us, and when we left, he followed us for a while. We thought it was just a coincidence, but now..."

Roger's mind raced. This could be the lead he needed. He looked at the kids, their faces filled with fear and determination. "Alright," he said finally, his voice firm. "But you stay close to me at all times. We do this together, and we do it carefully."

As they discussed their next steps, a sudden chill filled the room. The lights flickered, casting long, sinister shadows on the walls.

Roger's phone buzzed again. It was another message from the unknown number: "You can't escape the truth, Roger. It's closer than you think."

A sense of dread settled over them. Roger knew they were being watched, and the danger was far from over. The mystery deepened, and the stakes were higher than ever. They had to uncover the truth before it was too late.

The Shadows of Cincinnati

Griselda nodded. "I tried to keep him safe, but I failed. Now, it's up to us to finish what he started."

Griselda's arrival brought a new sense of urgency and hope to the group. She provided crucial leads that pointed to a larger conspiracy, connecting the dots between Lou's work and the broader network of corruption and crime.

Meanwhile, the children of the group members, who had been quietly observing from the side-lines, felt a growing sense of urgency. They had lost their parents to this dark mystery and were determined to uncover the truth. Each child, with their unique skills and perspectives, brought a new dimension to the investigation. Their youthful curiosity and determination added a layer of hope and resilience to the group's efforts.

Roger, sensing their isolation and fear, often took moments to comfort them. He would offer a reassuring smile, a gentle pat on the back, or a few encouraging words. "We're in this together," he would say, his voice filled with warmth. "We'll find the answers, and we'll do it as a team."

Determined to unmask the mole, Roger realized the note in Spanish held the key. He entered a URL from the note, revealing a fortified website. "Look at this! The statue of Timbuktum—everything points to it," Roger exclaimed, his eyes wide with revelation.

Marcos, skeptical, asked, "What could an ancient artifact in Ohio do to help us?"

Roger, his voice resolute, replied, "We both know about the strange murders. Lou's case is identical to the others. He was investigating a series of murders that seemed unrelated at first, but he found a pattern. All the victims were connected to a secret society that used the statue of Timbuktum as a symbol."

The group, now bound by a shared sense of dread and determination, prepared to face the unknown. The shadows of Cincinnati held many secrets, and they were about to uncover them all. As they left the archives, a cold wind howled through the streets, carrying with it the whispers of the past. The city's dark corners seemed to watch them, waiting for their next move. The truth was out there, lurking in the shadows, and it was more terrifying than they could have ever imagined. The night was thick with an eerie silence as the group gathered in the dimly lit hotel lobby. The air was heavy with unspoken fears, each member was lost in their thoughts. Among them were the children, who had lost their parents to the same dark forces they now sought to uncover. They believed that helping Roger solve Lou's murder would bring them closer to understanding who was after them and why their parents were killed. This mission was not just about justice for Lou; it was about finding answers to their own painful questions.

Roger, the de facto leader, paced back and forth, his mind racing with possibilities. The disappearance of Lou weighed heavily on them all, but it was Roger who felt the burden most acutely. He glanced at the children, their faces a mix of determination and fear. He knew they felt alone, thrust into a world of danger and uncertainty far too soon.

"Where do we start?" Jamie asked, her voice barely above a whisper. Her eyes darted around the room, as if expecting danger to leap from the shadows.

Roger paused, his gaze settling on the chief's office. "We start where Lou was last seen," he said, his voice firm. The group nodded in agreement, their resolve hardening.

They stepped into the cold night, the city's neon lights flickering ominously above them. The streets, usually bustling with activity, were eerily deserted. The chief's office loomed ahead, its windows dark and foreboding. Roger's car was conspicuously absent, replaced by a chilling note in Spanish taped to the door. Ian, with trembling hands, used his phone to translate: "Stay away from Lou's bloodshed. You are under surveillance. One mistake and you'll meet Lou."

A shiver ran down their spines as they absorbed the message. Roger, his face a mask of determination, quickly organized a taxi to the archives. "Cincinnati police, I have a warrant to investigate Lou Wojehowski's murder," he announced, his voice echoing in the stillness. They were heading to the archives to find any records or evidence that might shed light on Lou's disappearance and the broader conspiracy they were uncovering.

The ride to the archives was tense, each member of the group lost in their thoughts. The city lights blurred past, casting fleeting shadows on their faces. Marcos, a tall figure with a brooding presence, sat silently, his eyes sharp and searching. Ian, beside him, fidgeted nervously, his mind racing with possibilities. Jamie and Ada, their faces pale with fear, clung to each other for comfort. Paul, the youngest among them, sat quietly, his mind replaying the brief but impactful encounter he had with Lou.

Breaking the silence, Paul spoke up, and his voice tinged with a mix of sadness and determination. "I only met Lou once, but he left a strong impression. When he found me lost and scared, he took me to the hotel. On the way, he told me something I'll never forget. 'Paul, sometimes life can be tough, and it might feel like you're all alone. But remember, you have a light inside you that can guide you through the darkest times. Never let that light go out.'"

Roger glanced at Paul, his expression softening. "He said that?" Roger asked, his voice heavy with emotion.

Paul nodded. "Yeah, he did. He always had a way of making you feel safe and hopeful. I know you must be feeling a huge loss, Roger. I feel it too. Lou was an incredible person."

Roger placed a comforting hand on Paul's shoulder. "Thank you, Paul. Lou was special, and we'll honour his memory by finding the truth."

The derelict office loomed ahead, its shadowed corridors whispering secrets of dread. The group hesitated at the entrance, the weight of their mission pressing down on them. Roger took a deep breath and pushed the door open, the creak echoing through the empty halls.

Inside, the air was thick with dust and decay. The walls were lined with peeling wallpaper, and the floorboards creaked underfoot. Marcos and Ian scoured the area for clues, their flashlights cutting through the darkness. Jamie and Ada, their nerves on edge, found nothing but cobwebs and broken furniture. Paul, ever diligent despite his age, sifted through records until his hand brushed against something sinister—a suitcase with Lou's name on it. Inside, they found a bag of cocaine and a stash of cash.

"Roger! We've unearthed a nightmare," Ian called out, his voice barely above a whisper. Roger arrived, his eyes wide with disbelief. "Cocaine and cash, shrouded in secrecy. It can't be Lou, just can't be!"

Suddenly, the lights flickered, casting monstrous shadows that danced on the walls. A chilling gust swept through the room, slamming the door shut with a deafening bang. Frantic hands fumbled for flashlights, their beams revealing a figure looming in the darkness.

"Who's there?" Roger demanded, his voice steady despite the fear gnawing at his insides. The figure remained silent, then a soft tapping began, growing louder and more insistent. With desperation, they approached the desk. The tapping ceased, replaced by a low, menacing growl. The desk drawer flew open, revealing an antique music box and a note: "The truth lies not in what you find, but in what finds you."

Realizing they were the hunted, the group knew the game was far from over. As dawn's first light crept through the windows, they embarked on a relentless search for the truth. Paul, delving deeper into the files, uncovered a connection between William Oklahoma and Linda, casting a dark shadow over the Cincinnati syndicate. A whisper, barely audible, sent shivers down their spines: "They know too much. Silence them all." Among them lurked a mole, a spectre of betrayal.

Roger, seeking clarity, found the DNA evidence inconclusive. He had collected samples from the scene where Lou was last seen, hoping to find a match, but the results were frustratingly vague. Back in the archives, he scrutinized each member, but the mole was a master of disguise. "Trust is a luxury," Roger intoned, his voice heavy with the weight of their predicament. The tale twisted into a macabre tapestry of treachery and conspiracy. Lou's clandestine existence unfurled, leading them to a vault of secrets.

As they delved deeper into the archives, a shadowy figure appeared at the entrance. The group tensed, ready for another confrontation, but the figure stepped into the light, revealing herself to be Griselda, Lou's widow. She had been following their investigation closely, driven by her own need for answers and justice.

Griselda's eyes were red-rimmed, a testament to sleepless nights and endless worry. "I knew something was wrong," she began, her voice trembling slightly. "Lou had been acting strange for months. He was secretive, always looking over his shoulder. I found these files hidden in his study. They detail a conspiracy so vast, it's hard to believe."

She handed Roger a stack of documents. "Lou didn't tell me about this directly. I think he was trying to protect me, and maybe even you, Roger. He knew how dangerous this was. But I couldn't just stand by. I had to know what he was involved in."

Roger flipped through the files, his face growing more serious with each page. "Lou was onto something big," he muttered. "He was close to uncovering the truth, and that's why they got to him."

Beyond the Veil

The group had been tirelessly sifting through the files Griselda had given them, each document more perplexing than the last. They were desperate for any clue about Lou's fate, still grappling with the belief that he might be dead. It was during one late-night session, under the dim light of a flickering lamp, that they stumbled upon a peculiar note. This note, hidden within the folds of an old, yellowed file, contained cryptic chants and a ritual. The note was written in an ancient language, and at first, it seemed like just another dead end.

As they continued to study the files, Paul noticed that the symbols on the note matched those in an old, dusty book in the museum's restricted section. The book, bound in worn leather and filled with arcane symbols, had been overlooked for decades. Intrigued, Paul suggested they investigate further. "Paul, you might be right. We need everyone. Call them all. I'll get a car," Roger said, urgency in his voice.

Swiftly, they gathered the group and headed to the museum. The files had hinted at strange occurrences and unexplained phenomena, but it was the note that provided the final clue. As they squeezed through a narrow gap between dusty wooden planks and crawled through a grimy set of pipes to reach the hidden room where the book was found, the pieces of the puzzle began to fall into place.

Paul placed his hand on the statue and recited the mantra from the note, "Ham nay mo na may nya co Sen I Boch." As the words echoed through the room, the air shimmered, and the entire group saw a vivid image of Lou in a dimension that resembled a wasteland scrapyard. The note had mentioned a "Gaulnet," an ancient device resembling an old, rundown toaster with a screen displaying all the information about Lou. The group was stunned by the precision of the spell. "We have help on the inside," Paul thought. The Gaulnet revealed that Lou had been pulled into this dimension due to a rift caused by an experiment gone wrong, a tear in the fabric of reality itself. This was the moment they realized Lou wasn't dead but trapped in another dimension.

Roger's heart soared with happiness at the revelation that Lou was alive. The joy was palpable, but it was tinged with uncertainty. Could they really bring him back? These things only happened in books or movies, not in real life. The group exchanged nervous glances, their minds racing with the possibilities. If Lou was alive in another dimension, maybe their parents were too. The thought brought a glimmer of hope to their eyes.

"Paul, say the spells! We need to help Lou now," Roger urged frantically. Paul gripped the artifact with determination and chanted, "Jyo dun fa uh ji ja na ug ya." As the chant grew louder, the room around them began to warp and twist. Roger felt as if he were falling into a trance. Like the rest of the group, his drowsy eyes opened to the sight of them plummeting onto the island, landing flat on their faces.

As the group disembarked onto the new island, they were greeted by an eerie silence, broken only by the distant calls of exotic birds. The terrain was rugged, with dense underbrush and towering trees that seemed to touch the sky. Determined to find Roger's best friend, they split into smaller teams, each tasked with exploring different parts of the island. Marcos led his team through a narrow path, their senses heightened by the unfamiliar surroundings. The air was thick with humidity, and the ground beneath their feet was uneven and treacherous. Suddenly, they stumbled upon an ancient, overgrown ruin, its stone walls covered in moss and vines. Intrigued, they decided to investigate, hoping to find clues about their friend's whereabouts.

Meanwhile, Ian's team ventured towards the island's interior, where they encountered a series of cascading waterfalls. The sound of rushing water was both soothing and invigorating, providing a brief respite from their arduous journey. As they navigated the slippery rocks, they discovered a hidden cave behind one of the waterfalls. Inside, they found remnants of a campsite, suggesting that someone had been there recently.

Back at the beach, Jamie and Ada worked tirelessly to fortify their makeshift camp, ensuring they had a safe place to return to. They gathered firewood, set up a perimeter, and kept a vigilant watch for any signs of danger. As night fell and the group reconvened at their makeshift camp, they shared their discoveries and formulated a plan to rescue Roger's best friend, Lou. The remnants of the campsite in the hidden cave suggested that he might be on the island, possibly in need of help.

Marcos, taking charge, divided the group into two teams. One team, led by Ian, would return to the cave to search for more clues, while the other team, led by Marcos, would explore the ancient ruins they had discovered earlier. They hoped to find any signs or messages left behind by Lou. The next morning, the teams set out with renewed determination. Ian's team navigated the treacherous path back to the cave, carefully examining every nook and cranny for any indication of recent activity. They found a makeshift map etched into the cave wall, hinting at a hidden location deeper within the island.

Meanwhile, Marcos's team delved into the ruins, uncovering ancient artifacts and deciphering cryptic symbols. Among the relics, they discovered a journal that seemed to belong to Lou. The journal detailed his journey and hinted at a secret hideout where he might be waiting for rescue. With this newfound information, the teams regrouped and decided to follow the map and the journal's clues. The journey was arduous, filled with natural obstacles and the constant threat of wild animals. Yet, their resolve never wavered. After days of relentless searching, they finally reached a secluded part of the island, hidden from plain sight. There, they found

Lou, weak but alive, having survived on the island's resources.

The Rift of Despair

Lou's childhood was a harrowing ordeal. Born into a world of crime and narcotics, his father coerced him into trafficking drugs from a young age. The weight of responsibilities at home was crushing, and he was subjected to relentless beatings with a leather belt by his father. His small frame bore the scars of his father's cruelty, each mark a testament to his suffering. Lou's eyes, once bright with the innocence of youth, had grown dull and haunted. It was only his mother, despite her timidity and fear, who always found a way to console him. Yet, despite all her efforts, his father's dark shadow had deeply overclouded Lou's mind.

Eventually, his mother went missing. The day she disappeared, Lou's fragile world shattered. He broke down, consumed by a torrent of grief and despair. The one beacon of light in his dark existence was gone, leaving him utterly alone and lost.

One fateful day, a gang of delinquents ambushed him in a dark alley, intent on ending his life. Lou's heart pounded in his chest as he fought to escape, but the odds were against him. Just as he thought his end had come, a shadowy figure emerged from the darkness. A mafia member, drawn by the commotion, intervened and saved Lou. This mysterious saviour took Lou under his wing, grooming him as an apprentice in the underworld. The mafia became his new family, teaching him the art of survival in a world where trust was a luxury.

At 17, Lou's spirit, though battered, remained unbroken. He seized an opportunity to escape the clutches of the mafia, determined to pursue justice. His journey was fraught with challenges, but his resolve was unwavering. By 26, Lou had completed his education and joined the police force. His dedication and hard work earned him numerous promotions, and he became known for his relentless pursuit of justice. Yet, despite his success, the shadows of his past loomed large. He was haunted by the knowledge that the mafia would one day seek retribution.

That day came sooner than he had anticipated. The mafia, relentless in their pursuit, finally found him. They abducted Lou and subjected him to a horrifying experiment. Using advanced technology, they created a dimensional rift, trapping Lou in a parallel dimension. To cover their tracks, they left behind a lifelike replica of

Lou's body in the lake, making it appear as though he had died. This body was a perfect decoy, fooling everyone into believing Lou was gone forever.

In the parallel dimension, Lou's memory was erased, and he was reprogrammed to remember only the past two years. Though it had been merely two days on Earth, in the wasteland dimension, it felt like an eternity. The landscape was a desolate expanse, filled with twisted metal and the remnants of a once-thriving world. The sky was perpetually overcast, casting a gloomy pall over everything. The mafia transformed Lou into a cold, unfeeling operative, using him as a pawn in their sinister plans. His eyes, once filled with determination, now reflected a chilling emptiness.

Their master plan was now in motion. They had orchestrated events to ensnare a gang of children and Roger, meticulously monitoring them through a mole. The pieces of their sinister puzzle were finally coming together.

Echoes of Deceit

The night was still, the air heavy with unspoken fears. Lou sat by the campfire, staring into the flickering flames, his mind a labyrinth of confusion and fragmented memories. Roger, sensing his friend's turmoil, sat down beside him. The bond they shared was unspoken but profound, forged through countless trials and tribulations.

"Hey, Lou," Roger began softly, his voice a soothing balm. "Do you remember the time we snuck out of school to go fishing? You caught that huge trout, and we had to hide it from the principal."

Lou's brow furrowed as he tried to grasp the memory. It was like trying to catch smoke with his bare hands. "I... I don't know, Roger. Everything's so hazy."

Roger placed a reassuring hand on Lou's shoulder. "It's okay, buddy. We'll figure this out together. Remember the summer we spent at the lake? We built that raft and sailed it across, even though it was barely holding together."

A flicker of recognition sparked in Lou's eyes. "The lake... I remember the lake. We almost drowned, but we laughed about it later."

"That's right," Roger said, his voice filled with warmth. "And what about the time we camped out in the backyard, telling ghost stories until we scared ourselves silly?"

Lou's eyes widened as more memories began to surface. "I remember that! You told the story about the headless horseman, and I couldn't sleep for a week."

Roger chuckled, the sound rich with nostalgia. "Yeah, and you swore you'd never listen to another ghost story again. But you always did."

The memories flowed like a river, each one bringing Lou closer to the person he once was. Tears welled up in his eyes as he looked at Roger. "I remember, Roger. I remember everything."

Roger pulled Lou into a tight embrace, their bond stronger than ever. "Welcome back, Lou. We missed you."

As Roger walked away, Lou's smile faded. His mind was a storm of conflicting emotions. He had been struggling with his memory, but the truth was far darker. Lou was working with the mob, a ruthless group that promised to reveal the whereabouts of his mother if he led Roger and the kids into their trap.

Lou's thoughts raced. I can't believe I'm doing this. But I have no choice. They promised to tell me where my mother is. If I don't lead Roger and the kids into their trap, I'll never see them again. He looked at his friends, feeling a pang of guilt. They trust me. They have no idea I'm leading them to their doom.

As the first light of dawn pierced the horizon, the group stirred from their slumber with the urgency of their mission weighing heavily on their minds. Lou, wide awake, was tormented by his hidden agenda. He had moments of doubt, questioning the morality of his actions. The bond he shared with Roger, forged through countless trials, weighed heavily on his conscience.

"Morning, everyone," Roger greeted, his voice steady and reassuring. "We need to figure out how to get out of this dimension. Any ideas?"

Marcos, stretching and yawning, joined the circle around the campfire. "We need to find some clues or signs that can lead us out. Maybe there's something in the forest we haven't discovered yet."

Jamie, who had been unusually quiet, looked up with tear-filled eyes. "I miss my parents," she whispered, her voice breaking. "I don't know if we'll ever see them again."

The group fell silent, the weight of their collective grief settling over them. Each of them, except for Lou and Roger, had lost their parents. The pain was a shared burden, a bond forged in sorrow.

Roger knelt beside Jamie, his heart aching for the young girl. "I know it's hard, Jamie. We all miss our loved ones. But we have to stay strong for them and for each other. We'll find a way out of here, I promise."

Lou watched as Roger comforted Jamie, his friend's pure heart shining through. Despite his own dark intentions, Lou couldn't help but feel a pang of admiration for Roger's unwavering courage and compassion.

"Roger's right," Lou said, his voice steady. "We need to stick together and keep moving forward. We'll find a way out of this, I know we will."

The group packed up their camp, their bond evident in the way they worked seamlessly together. They fashioned makeshift weapons by tying sharp stones to logs, preparing for any dangers they might encounter. As they ventured deeper into the forest, they stumbled upon a cabin in the distance.

"Guys, a cabin! We can stay there," Lou suggested. They made their way to the cabin just as darkness enveloped the land. Setting up a fire, they settled into the eerie shelter. As they sat by the campfire, Lou's resolve wavered. The sight of his friends, laughing and sharing stories, made him question his loyalty to the mob. But the hope of finding his mother was a powerful motivator. He knew he had to follow through with the plan, no matter the cost.

Lou's thoughts were a whirlwind of fear and guilt. His memory was never lost; it was a ruse to gain their trust. The mob had given him a clear directive: lead the kids into a trap, and then they would reveal his mothers' location. The weight of his mission bore down on him, suffocating him with its darkness. He had to lead them all eventually, or he would never see his mother again.

I can't believe I'm doing this, Lou thought, his mind racing. These people are my friends. Roger saved my life more times than I can count. How can I betray them like this? But the image of his mother, lost and possibly suffering, loomed large in his mind. He had no choice. The mob's reach was long and their promises were real. If he didn't follow through, he might never find his mother.

Lou questioned his choices, his conscience battling with his fear. Maybe there's another way. Maybe I can warn them, help them escape. But deep down, he knew the mob would find out. They always did. And the consequences would be dire.

As he looked at his friends, the guilt gnawed at him. They trust me. They have no idea I'm leading them to their doom. But I have to do it. I have to find my mother. No matter the cost.

Suddenly, a hand clamped over Paul's mouth, stifling his scream. Emerging from the shadows was Paul's doppelgänger. To their horror, each member's twin rose from the ground, intent on annihilating them. The ensuing battle was brutal and chaotic. Each doppelgänger mirrored their counterpart's moves with uncanny precision, leading to a vicious and bloody struggle. Roger was slashed across the arm, Jamie took a blow to the head, and Ada narrowly avoided a fatal stab. The forest echoed with the sounds of clashing weapons and pained cries. It was in the midst of this savage melee that Roger, through the haze of pain and adrenaline, noticed a crucial detail: the doppelgängers could only fight their own counterparts.

"They can only fight their own doppelgänger. Switch opponents now!" Roger shouted. In a swift, coordinated move, they ducked and swapped adversaries. Roger, with fierce determination, rammed and stabbed the doppelgängers with his spear. One by one, the sinister doubles turned to dust, leaving the group breathless but safe.

Lou, meanwhile, moved through the chaos with a calculated detachment. He swung his weapon, but his strikes were deliberately off-target, missing the doppelgängers by inches. His eyes darted around, searching for any sign of his parents, any clue that might lead him to them. His heart pounded with fear and guilt, but he steeled himself, knowing he had to see this through.

As Roger fought valiantly, Lou's actions became more sinister. He "accidentally" tripped Jamie, causing her to fall into the path of a doppelgänger. She screamed as the creature loomed over her, but Roger intervened just in time, slashing the doppelgänger with a fierce cry. Lou's heart twisted with guilt, but he forced himself to remain focused on his goal.

The battle raged on, gruesome and relentless. Blood splattered the ground, and the air was thick with the stench of fear and death. Lou's mind was a storm of conflicting emotions. He wanted to save Roger, but he had no choice but to ensure the kids died. His strikes were half-hearted, his movements sluggish, as he wrestled with his conscience.

Roger, sensing something was off, glanced at Lou with suspicion. But in the heat of battle, he had no time to dwell on it. He fought with all his might, his determination unwavering. He saved Marcos from a deadly blow, pulled Ada out of harm's way, and shielded Ian from a vicious attack. His actions were heroic, driven by a fierce loyalty to his friends.

As the last doppelgänger fell, turning to dust, the group collapsed in exhaustion. Lou, panting and covered in sweat, forced a smile. "We did it," he said, his voice hollow. "We survived."

Roger looked at him, his eyes narrowing. Something about Lou's demeanour seemed off, but he couldn't put his finger on it. He shrugged it off, attributing it to the stress of the battle. "Yeah, we did," he replied, though his tone was wary.

Lou took the credit for the victory, his heart heavy with deceit. He had played his part, but the guilt gnawed at him. He had betrayed his friends, led them into a trap, and now he had to live with the consequences. As they regrouped and prepared for the next leg of their journey, the atmosphere was thick with tension. The forest around them seemed to close in, shadows dancing menacingly in the flickering firelight. Roger, ever the leader, began to strategize their next move, his mind racing with plans to keep everyone safe. Lou, on the other hand, stood apart, his thoughts a chaotic whirl of guilt and determination. He had taken credit for the victory, but the hollow praise only deepened his inner turmoil.

Roger's eyes lingered on Lou, a flicker of doubt crossing his mind. Something about Lou's actions during the fight didn't sit right with him, but he couldn't afford to dwell on it now. They had to keep moving, had to find a way out of this nightmare. As the group gathered their belongings and steeled themselves for whatever horrors lay ahead, Lou's resolve hardened. He would find his mother, no matter the cost. But as he glanced at his friends, a pang of regret pierced his heart. He knew that the true battle was just beginning, and the choices he made would haunt him forever.

Descent into Darkness

As they ventured deeper into the wasteland, an unsettling feeling crept over them, sending chills down their spines. The barren landscape seemed to whisper secrets, the wind howling like a distant wail. The group, led by Roger, a tall figure with a rugged face etched by countless battles, moved cautiously. His eyes, sharp and vigilant, scanned the surroundings for any signs of danger.

Lou, with his piercing blue eyes and a demeanour that masked his inner turmoil, followed closely. His thoughts churned with a sinister satisfaction as he reflected on the unfolding plan. "Everything is proceeding as it should," he mused darkly. "The map was expertly planted. They may have survived my previous attempts, but how did they manage to defeat the doppelgängers?" He chuckled to himself. "No matter. Once I lead them into the mafia's base, their heads will roll in no time."

Suddenly, they stumbled upon a dilapidated cabin, its exterior plastered with ominous notes: "Do not enter," "Those who enter do not return," and "If you are human, you will never leave." The sight of the cabin sent a shiver down their spines.

Roger's curiosity was piqued. "We must enter; these are signs of life, written in human blood," he mused, his eyes narrowing. With a forceful push, he banged open the cabin door. The rusty hinges groaned, revealing a room filled with papers and a map marked with an exit. Disturbing notes littered the floor, detailing the grim fates of previous visitors. Each note bore the name and severed head of a victim, a macabre testament to the cabin's sinister history.

The map suggested a perilous journey back home, a path fraught with dangers that could easily claim their lives. Realizing the urgency of their situation, they knew they had to act swiftly if they wanted to see Earth again. The clock was ticking, and the wasteland held more secrets than they had ever imagined.

"Guys, what are we waiting for? Let's go," Marcos prompted, breaking Lou's reverie. The map's route led them through a perilous mountain hike and a grueling 19-kilometer trek across a desert. The group, armed and determined, nodded in agreement, ready to embark on the arduous journey home.

The mountains demanded every ounce of their strength, requiring them to scale steep inclines and make daring leaps across chasms. The rocky terrain was treacherous, with loose stones and jagged edges threatening to send them tumbling into the abyss below. As they climbed, the air grew thin and cold, their breaths visible in the frosty air. Each step was a battle against gravity, their muscles burning with exertion. Suddenly, a wild baboon appeared, its eyes gleaming with malice. Before they could react, it called forth an entire army of baboons, which descended upon the group with terrifying speed. They ran for their lives, the baboons hot on their heels.

"I know what they want! Barricade the climbing paths and give them a bit of food!" Ada screamed, her voice cutting through the chaos. Marcos, acting quickly, did as instructed. The baboons halted, distracted by the food. The group reached the summit, where they collected precious water and food, and began the final stretch of their journey.

The desert trek was even more grueling. The sun beat down mercilessly, turning the sand into a scorching sea of heat. Each step felt like walking on hot coals, their feet sinking into the soft sand, making progress agonizingly slow. The landscape was a vast, empty expanse, with no shade or shelter in sight. Fatigue, dehydration, and starvation gnawed at them over the next few days. Their supplies dwindled rapidly, and sleep became their worst adversary. The nights were freezing, the temperature dropping drastically, leaving them shivering and exhausted. Yet, they pressed on, driven by the hope of reaching home. Finally, they stood before what appeared to be a gateway to salvation—or was it?

Lou's demeanour had shifted dramatically. Where once there was a glimmer of hope in his eyes, now there was a cold, calculating edge. It all started when he stumbled upon an old, tattered photograph hidden in the cabin they had explored. The image was of his mother, standing in front of a house he didn't recognize. Scrawled on the back were the words, "I'll find you, no matter what."

This discovery ignited a spark of hope within Lou. He became obsessed with the idea that his mother was still alive, out there somewhere, searching for him. But as days turned into weeks, and weeks into months, the hope began to twist into something darker. The constant disappointment and the harsh reality of his situation made him bitter. He started to see the other kids as obstacles, reminders of his own helplessness.

Blood and Betrayal

The group had been wandering through the desolate wasteland for days, their spirits worn thin by the relentless sun and the eerie silence that surrounded them. It was during one of these aimless treks that they stumbled upon a set of faint tracks, barely visible in the dust. Roger, ever the vigilant leader, followed the trail with a sense of urgency, his instincts telling him it might lead to something significant.

As they pressed on, the tracks grew clearer, leading them to an old, abandoned warehouse on the outskirts of a forgotten town. The building loomed ahead, a monolithic structure shrouded in darkness. Shadows danced on the walls, cast by the flickering light of a single, swinging bulb. The air was thick with tension, the kind that prickled the skin and set nerves on edge. Roger, Marcos, Ian, Jamie, Ada, and Paul stood together, their faces etched with determination and fear. They were ready for the fight of their lives.

Lou, however, stood apart, a smirk playing on his lips as he aligned himself with William, the Mafia and his mob. The betrayal was a knife to Roger's heart, twisting deeper with every passing second.

William, infamously dubbed "the Sinister," was a mafia boss whose reign was marked by unparalleled ruthlessness and strategic brilliance. His dark legacy was etched in power struggles and an unyielding grip over his domain. Known for his sharp intellect and ability to outwit his foes, William's very name instilled fear and commanded respect among those who encountered him.

Roger's eyes narrowed as he looked at Lou. "I can't believe you're with them, Lou. After everything we've been through."

Lou's expression was cold, his eyes devoid of the warmth they once held. "You don't understand, Roger. This is bigger than all of us."

Roger's voice trembled with a mix of anger and hurt. "Bigger than us? We were a family, Lou. We trusted you."

Lou's eyes flickered with a moment of doubt, but he quickly masked it. "Trust? You think trust matters in a world like this? It's about survival."

Roger's voice grew more desperate. "Survival? Is that what you call this? Betraying your friends for what? Power? Safety?"

Lou's smirk faded, replaced by a hardened resolve. "You don't get it, Roger. William promised me something you never could. He promised me my mother."

Roger's eyes widened in shock. "Your mother? Lou, she's gone. William is using you!"

William's laughter echoed through the warehouse, cold and menacing. "Oh, Roger, you naive fool. Lou's mother is very much alive. William's laughter turned into a sinister grin as he looks at Lou, "and so is his father."

"My father... alive? This can't be true," he whispered, his mind reeling from the revelation. The ground seemed to shift beneath him as the weight of the truth settled in.

"Oh and not to forget, Roger, so are your parents. Or at least, they were."

Roger's heart sank. "What do you mean?"

William's eyes gleamed with malice. "We needed leverage, you see. The fan meet-up was the perfect opportunity. We took the kids parents to ensure you'd all come running. And now, you're here, just as planned."

Roger's voice broke with anguish. "You monster! You killed them!"

William shrugged nonchalantly. "Collateral damage. They were in the way. Just like you are now."

William wanted the kids dead because they were the last loose ends in his sinister plan. Their parents had been a threat to his operations, and eliminating them was necessary to maintain control, they knew too much and were all planning on exposing William and his sinister operation. The kids, potential avengers, had to be dealt with to ensure no one would come after him.

The tension was palpable, a tangible force that seemed to crackle in the air. Without warning, the two sides clashed. Fists flew, and the sound of punches landing echoed through the cavernous space. Marcos and Ian took on two of William's henchmen, their movements swift and precise. Marcos delivered a powerful uppercut, sending one henchman sprawling, while Ian dodged a punch and countered with a swift kick to the ribs. Jamie and Ada fought back-to-back, their movements synchronized. Jamie blocked a punch aimed at Ada and retaliated with a spinning kick, while Ada disarmed another attacker with a swift twist of her wrist, sending the weapon clattering to the ground.

William laughed, his voice dripping with contempt. "You think you can beat me? You're nothing but a bunch of misfits!"

Roger charged at William, but Lou intercepted him, their fists colliding in a flurry of blows. Paul tried to help, but was quickly overwhelmed by another mob member. He grappled with his opponent, using his strength to throw him against a stack of crates.

Roger struggled against Lou. "Lou, snap out of it! This isn't you!"

William watched with a sneer, his eyes gleaming with malice. "Look at you, Roger. Pathetic. You always were the weakest link."

Lou hesitated, William's words cutting through the chaos. He glanced at Roger, who was now on the ground, struggling to get up.

William's voice was mocking. "You're all worthless. Especially you, Roger. Always dragging everyone down."

Roger was on the ground, blood trickling from a cut on his forehead. He tried to get up, but William kicked him back down, laughing cruelly. "Stay down, Roger. You're not worth the effort."

Lou's eyes widened as he saw Roger's life hanging by a thread. Something snapped inside him. He saw the pain in Roger's eyes, the betrayal. Anger surged through him, and he turned on William, his fists clenched.

"Shut up, William! You definitely don't know about us!" Lou attacked William with a newfound fury, catching him off guard. He landed a series of rapid punches, driving William back. The rest of the gang noticed the shift and rallied, fighting with renewed vigour.

Marcos and Ian fought with a renewed intensity, their movements a blur of fists and feet. Marcos delivered a devastating roundhouse kick, while Ian used a discarded pipe to fend off two attackers at once. Jamie and Ada moved like a well-oiled machine, their attacks coordinated and relentless. Jamie landed a powerful punch that sent an attacker crashing into a wall, while Ada used a series of quick jabs to incapacitate another.

Paul, seeing Lou's change of heart, fought with renewed determination. He tackled a mob member to the ground, delivering a series of punishing blows. The warehouse was a whirlwind of chaos, but they were gaining the upper hand.

Just as it seemed they might win, William pulled out a hidden knife and lunged at Roger. Lou tried to intercept, but he was too late. The blade sank into Roger's side, and he fell to the ground, blood pooling around him.

Roger's voice was weak and breathless. "Guys... keep fighting... don't let him win..."

The gang fought harder, driven by Roger's sacrifice. Lou, filled with rage and guilt, delivered a final, devastating blow to William, knocking him out cold.

The warehouse fell silent, the fight over. The gang gathered around Roger, their faces etched with grief.

Marcos choked back tears. "We did it, Roger. We won."

Roger smiled weakly, his eyes closing.

As Roger's breathing slowed, the gang held him close, their victory tinged with sorrow. Lou knelt beside him, tears streaming down his face.

"I'm so sorry, Roger. I should have never doubted you," Lou whispered.

Final Reckoning

The victory was theirs, but at a devastating cost. Roger lay lifeless, and the group stood around him, their grief palpable in the cold, desolate air. The warehouse, once a battleground, now echoed with the silence of loss.

Lou, his voice breaking, whispered, "The rift back home is in this building. We must carry Roger's body back." His words hung heavy in the air, a grim reminder of their reality.

With tears streaming down their faces, they lifted Roger from the pool of blood. Lou, moving with a precision born of desperation, led the way to the rift. In an instant, they were back in the museum, the transition so seamless it felt as though mere minutes had passed since their departure.

The next morning, Roger was laid to rest in a casket, honored as the hero he was. The victory brought no joy, only a profound sense of grief. Lou, hollow and broken, had watched Roger die right before his eyes.

Outside the funeral, in a shadowy, dilapidated building, a masked man with a hood stood before a wall of flickering screens. Each screen displayed footage of the wasteland, though most flashed error messages. His eyes, cold and calculating, scanned the images with a sinister intensity.

"William has died to these traitors, and Lou, my son, you have betrayed me for the last time!" he raged, his voice echoing through the empty halls. The screens beeped ominously as they zoomed in on Roger's lifeless form. William's vitals were flat; he was dead. The building, now in shambles, bore silent witness to the chaos.

The masked man turned, his hoodie emblazoned with the logo of Beastly Gaming. He entered a hidden arsenal, a room filled with jet packs, guns, and war machines. Donning a suit of armour, he emerged, his rage palpable.

Unaware of the looming threat, the gang mourned their fallen friend. Lou, wracked with guilt and sorrow, vowed to protect his friends and honour Roger's memory. But as the masked man prepared for his next move, the gang's victory felt hollow, a prelude to an even greater battle.

The masked man, now fully armoured, stood atop a hill overlooking the city. "This is just the beginning," he muttered, his voice filled with menace. "They will pay for their defiance."

As the sun set, casting long shadows over the city, the gang gathered at Roger's grave, their hearts heavy with loss. Lou placed a hand on the tombstone, his resolve hardening. "We will fight, Roger. We will fight for you."

The masked man watched from afar, his eyes burning with hatred. "Let the games begin," he whispered, a sinister smile spreading across his face.

www.ingramcontent.com/pod-product-compliance
Lightning Source LLC
Chambersburg PA
CBHW031322130726

47988CB00007B/2938